TO YOUR GOOD HEALTH

To Your Good Health

A RUSSIAN FOLK TALE

FROM THE ANDREW LANG VERSION

Illustrated by Mehlli Gobhai

Holiday House • New York

Printed in the United States of America

Library of Congress Cataloging in Publication Data
Main entry under title.

To your good health.

SUMMARY: A wily shepherd escapes death three times and finally gets the king to grant his wish.
[1. Folklore–Russia] I. Gobhai, Mehlli, illus.
PZ8.1.T5 398.2'2'0947 72–92580
ISBN 0–8234–0226–6

For Ada E. Jackson and Betty Miller

LONG, long ago there lived a king who was such a mighty monarch that whenever he sneezed everyone in the whole country had to say "To your good health!" Everyone said it except the shepherd with the solemn stare, and he would not say it.

The king heard of this and was very angry and sent for the shepherd to appear before him.

The shepherd came and stood before the throne, where the king sat looking very grand and powerful. But however grand or powerful he might be the shepherd did not feel a bit afraid of him.

"Say at once, 'To my good health!' " cried the king.

"To my good health!" replied the shepherd.

"To mine—to *mine*, you rascal, you vagabond!" stormed the king.

"To mine, to *mine*, your Majesty," was the answer.

"But to *mine*—to my own!" roared the king and beat on his breast in a rage.

"Well, yes; to mine, of course, to my own," cried the shepherd and gently tapped his breast.

The king was beside himself with fury and did not know what to do, when the Lord Chamberlain interfered:

"Say at once—say this very moment: 'To your health, your Majesty'; for if you don't say it you'll lose your life," he whispered.

"No, I won't say it till I get the princess for my wife," was the shepherd's answer. Now the princess was sitting on a little throne beside the king, her father, and she looked as sweet and lovely as a little golden dove. When she heard what the shepherd said she could not help laughing, for there is no denying the fact that this young shepherd with the solemn stare pleased her very much; indeed he pleased her better than any king's son she had yet seen.

But the king was not as pleasant as his daughter, and he gave orders to throw the shepherd into the white bear's pit.

The guards led him away and thrust him into the pit with the white bear, who had had nothing to eat for two days and was very hungry. The door of the pit was hardly closed when the bear rushed at the shepherd; but when it saw his eyes it was so frightened that it was ready to eat itself.

It shrank away into a corner and gazed at him from there and, in spite of being so famished, did not dare to touch him, but sucked his own paws from sheer hunger. The shepherd felt that if he once removed his eyes off the beast he was a dead man, and in order to keep himself awake he made songs and sang them, and so the night went by.

Next morning the Lord Chamberlain came to see the shepherd's bones and was amazed to find him alive and well.

He led him to the king, who fell into a furious passion and said: "Well, you have learned what it is to be very near death, and *now* will you say 'To my good health'?"

But the shepherd answered: "I am not afraid of ten deaths! I will only say it if I may have the princess for my wife."

"Then go to your death!" cried the king, and ordered him to be thrown into the den with the wild boars.

The wild boars had not been fed for a week, and when the shepherd was thrust into their den they rushed at him to tear him to pieces. But the shepherd took a little flute out of the sleeve of his jacket and began to play a merry tune, on which the wild boars first of all shrank shyly away and then got up on their hind legs and danced gaily. The shepherd would have given anything to be able to laugh, they looked so funny; but he dared not stop playing, for he knew well enough that the moment he stopped they would fall upon him and tear him to pieces. His eyes were of no use to him here, for he could not have stared ten wild boars in the face at once; so he kept on playing, and the wild boars danced very slowly, as if in a minuet; then by degrees he played faster and faster till they could hardly twist and turn quickly enough, and ended by all falling over each other in a heap, quite exhausted and out of breath.

Then the shepherd ventured to laugh at last; and he laughed so long and so loud that when the Lord Chamberlain came early in the morning, expecting to find only his bones, the tears were still running down his cheeks from laughter.

As soon as the king was dressed the shepherd was again brought before him; but he was more angry than ever to think the wild boars had not torn the man to bits, and he said: "Well, you have

learned what it feels to be near ten deaths. *Now* say 'To my good health!' "

But the shepherd broke in with, "I do not fear a hundred deaths, and I will only say it if I may have the princess for my wife."

"Then go to a hundred deaths!" roared the king and ordered the shepherd to be thrown down the deep vault of scythes.

The guards dragged him away to a dark dungeon, in the middle of which was a deep well with sharp scythes all around it. At the bottom of the well was a little light by which one could see whether anyone who was thrown in had fallen to the bottom.

When the shepherd was dragged to the dungeon he begged the guards to leave him alone a little while that he might look down into the pit of scythes; perhaps he might after all make up his mind to say "To your good health" to the king. So the guards left him alone and he stuck his long crook near the well, hung his cloak round the crook and put his hat on the top. He also hung his knapsack up inside the cloak so that it might seem to have some body within it. When this was done he called out to the guards and said that he had considered the matter but after all he could not make up his mind to say what the king wished. The guards came in, threw the hat and cloak, knapsack and crook all down the well together, watched to see how they put out the light at the bottom and came away, thinking that now there really was an end of the shepherd. But he had hidden in a dark corner and was merrily laughing to himself.

Quite early next morning came the Lord Chamberlain, carrying a lamp, and he nearly fell backwards with surprise when he saw the shepherd alive and well. He brought him to the king, whose fury was greater than ever, but who cried:

"Well, now you have been near a hundred deaths; will you say: 'To your good health'?"

But the shepherd only gave the same answer:

"I won't say it till the princess is my wife."

"Perhaps after all you may do it for less," said the king, who saw that there was no chance of making away with the shepherd; and he ordered

the state coach to be got ready. Then he made the shepherd get in with him and sit beside him and ordered the coachman to drive to the silver wood. When they reached it he said: "Do you see this silver wood? Well, if you will say, 'To your good health,' I will give it to you."

The shepherd turned hot and cold by turns, but he still persisted:

"I will not say it till the princess is my wife."

The king was much vexed; he drove further on till they came to a splendid castle, all of gold, and then he said:

"Do you see this golden castle? Well, I will give you that too, the silver wood and the golden castle, if only you will say that one thing to me: 'To your good health.' "

The shepherd gaped and wondered and was quite dazzled, but he still said:

"No, I will *not* say it till I have the princess for my wife."

This time the king was overwhelmed with grief and gave orders to drive on to the diamond pond, and there he tried once more.

"Do you see this diamond pond? I will give you that too, the silver wood and the golden castle and the diamond pond. You shall have them all—all—if you will but say: 'To your good health.' "

The shepherd had to shut his staring eyes tight not to be dazzled with the brilliant pond, but still he said:

"No, no; I will not say it till I have the princess for my wife."

Then the king saw that all his efforts were useless and that he might as well give in, so he said:

"Well, well, it's all the same to me—I will give you my daughter to wife; but, then, you really and truly must say to me: 'To your good health'."

"Of course I'll say it; why should I not say it? It stands to reason that I shall say it then."

At this the king was more delighted than anyone could have believed. He made it known all through the country that there were to be great rejoicings, as the princess was going to be married. And everyone rejoiced to think that the princess, who had refused so many royal suitors, should have ended by falling in love with the solemn-eyed shepherd.

There was such a wedding as had never been seen. Everyone ate and drank and danced. Even the sick were feasted, and quite tiny new-born children had presents given them.

But the greatest merry-making was in the king's palace; there the best bands played and the best food was cooked. A crowd of people sat down to table, and all was fun and merry-making.

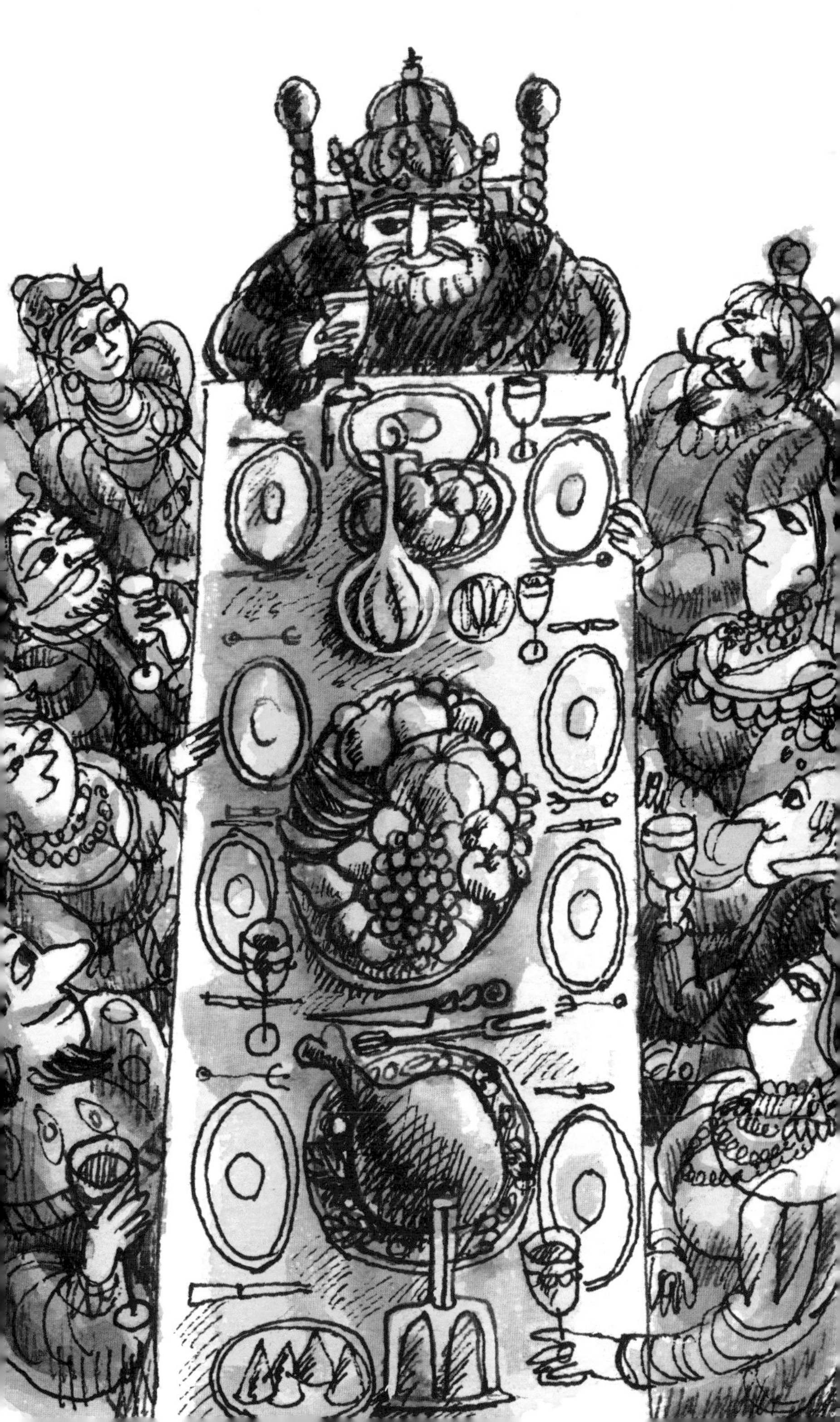

And when the groomsman, according to custom, brought in the great boar's head on a big dish and placed it before the king so that he might carve it and give everyone a share, the savory smell was so strong that the king began to sneeze with all his might.

"To your very good health!" cried the shepherd before anyone else, and the king was so delighted that he did not regret having given him his daughter.

In time, when the old king died, the shepherd succeeded him. He made a very good king and never expected his people to wish him well against their will; but, all the same everyone did wish him well, because they loved him.